Dear Parents:

Congratulations! Your child is taking the first steps on an exciting journey. The destination? Independent reading

D0469451

STEP INTO READING® will help your child get there. The program offers five steps to reading success. Each step includes fun stories and colorful art or photographs. In addition to original fiction and books with favorite characters, there are Step into Reading Non-Fiction Readers, Phonics Readers and Boxed Sets, Sticker Readers, and Comic Readers—a complete literacy program with something to interest every child.

Learning to Read, Step by Step!

Ready to Read   Preschool–Kindergarten
• big type and easy words • rhyme and rhythm • picture clues
For children who know the alphabet and are eager to begin reading.

Reading with Help   Preschool–Grade 1
• basic vocabulary • short sentences • simple stories
For children who recognize familiar words and sound out new words with help.

Reading on Your Own   Grades 1–3
• engaging characters • easy-to-follow plots • popular topics
For children who are ready to read on their own.

Reading Paragraphs   Grades 2–3
• challenging vocabulary • short paragraphs • exciting stories
For newly independent readers who read simple sentences with confidence.

Ready for Chapters   Grades 2–4
• chapters • longer paragraphs • full-color art
For children who want to take the plunge into chapter books but still like colorful pictures.

STEP INTO READING® is designed to give every child a successful reading experience. The grade levels are only guides; children will progress through the steps at their own speed, developing confidence in their reading. The F&P Text Level on the back cover serves as another tool to help you choose the right book for your child.

Remember, a lifetime love of reading starts with a single step!

For my ever-lovely wife, Renée —D.A.A.

For Marston —S.R.

Text copyright © 2018 by David A. Adler
Cover art and interior illustrations copyright © 2018 by Sam Ricks

All rights reserved. Published in the United States by Random House Children's Books, a division of Penguin Random House LLC, New York. Originally published in hardcover in the United States by Penguin Young Readers, an imprint of Penguin Random House LLC, New York, in 2018.

Step into Reading, Random House, and the Random House colophon are registered trademarks of Penguin Random House LLC.

Visit us on the Web!
StepIntoReading.com
rhcbooks.com

Educators and librarians, for a variety of teaching tools, visit us at
RHTeachersLibrarians.com

Library of Congress Cataloging-in-Publication Data is available upon request.
ISBN 978-0-593-43256-3 (trade) — ISBN 978-0-593-43257-0 (lib. bdg.)

Printed in the United States of America
10 9 8 7 6 5 4 3 2

This book has been officially leveled by using the F&P Text Level Gradient™ Leveling System.

KICK IT, MO!

by David A. Adler

illustrated by Sam Ricks

Random House 🏠 New York

"Kick it! Kick the ball!"

Mo Jackson calls out.

Mo kicks his desk.

"Kick it! Kick the ball!"

Mo kicks his bed.

"Kick it! Kick the ball!"

Mo kicks his pillow.

The pillow flies

into the hall.

Crash!

"Hey! You knocked over some books," his mother tells him.

"I'm sorry," Mo says.

"But I need to practice.

I have a soccer game today.

I need to kick, kick, kick."

Mo and his mother and father
pick up the books.
They all go outside.
Mo's mother rolls a soccer ball
and Mo kicks it.

But he kicks it

high into the air.

"Kick it low,"

his father tells him.

"Kick it on the ground."

Mo kicks the ball again.

It flies behind him.

Mo's mom and dad roll the
ball again and again.

Mo kicks it again and again.

But mostly he does not kick it

on the ground.

They all go to the soccer field.

Mo's team is the Billy Goats.

They are playing the Pups.

Mo is smaller and younger

than all the other players.

Coach Judy tells Mo's team,

"Keep the ball low.

Kick it on the ground.

Kick it toward the goal."

Tweet! Tweet!

The game starts.

The other team, the Pups,

has the ball.

A big Pups player

kicks it hard.

The ball speeds past Mo.

Mo chases after it.

A big Billy Goats player

kicks it the other way.

Mo stops.

He turns.

He runs the

other way.

The ball goes one way.

It goes the other way.

Mo runs after the ball.

He runs back and forth.

At last Mo stops.

He is tired.

The game is almost over.

The score is tied

zero to zero.

Mo is very close to the Pups' goal.

The ball stops by Mo.

"Kick the ball!

Kick the ball!"

Coach Judy shouts.

Mo pulls his foot back.

He is about to kick the ball.

A big Pups player

gets in front of Mo and kicks it.

Mo watches the ball
speed down the field toward
the Billy Goats' goal.
Mo is too tired
to chase it.

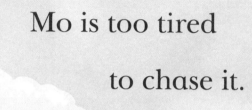

A Pups player kicks the ball right at the goal.

The Billy Goats goalie catches it.

She throws it back onto the field.

No score!

A Billy Goats player kicks

the ball hard.

It rolls toward the goal.

"Yes!" Mo shouts.

He thinks his team will score.

But the Pups goalie stops it.

He throws it hard.

He throws it right at Mo.

Mo pulls his foot way back.

It's a mighty kick.

The Pups goalie jumps.

But Mo's mighty kick

mostly misses the ball.

The ball rolls slowly into the goal.

"Yes!" Coach Judy shouts.

"Goal!" Billy Goats players shout.

Tweet! Tweet!

The game is over.

The Billy Goats win one to zero.

"Mo! Mo! Mo!"

the Billy Goats shout.

Mo tells Coach Judy,

"But I missed my kick."

Coach Judy says,

"You fooled the goalie.

He jumped for a hard, high kick,

but you kept the ball on the

ground."

"Mo! Mo! Mo!"

his mother and father cheer

on their way home.

"Our Mo won the game."